Anna Seward

Llangollen Vale With Other Poems

Anna Seward

Llangollen Vale With Other Poems

ISBN/EAN: 9783744716123

Printed in Europe, USA, Canada, Australia, Japan

Cover: Foto ©Andreas Hilbeck / pixelio.de

More available books at **www.hansebooks.com**

LLANGOLLEN VALE,

WITH

OTHER POEMS:

BY

ANNA SEWARD.

LONDON:

PRINTED FOR G. SAEL, NO. 192, STRAND.

1796.

SONNET.

DEVA, when next my vagrant fteps explore
　　The haunts romantic, where thy filver ftreams,
　　On which the garifh Sun but feldom gleams,
　　Fill with their wild and fancy-foothing roar,
LLANGOLLEN's verdant ftraights, and mountains hoar,
　　How fhall I dwell enraptur'd on the themes,
　　That now th' immortal MUSE of Britain deems
　　Worthy her facred fcroll, unmark'd before!
The Steeds whofe fetlocks fwam in blood, the hoft
　　Of GLENDOUR, claiming Valour's brighteft meed,
　　HOEL's love-breathing harp, and lays divine,
And the fair WANDERERS from Ierne's coaft,
　　Who, to fond Friendfhip's gentle power decreed,
　　Rear in thy hallow'd Vale the fimple fhrine.

H. F. CARY.

CANNOCK, *December*, 1795.

A

LLANGOLLEN VALE,

INSCRIBED TO

THE RIGHT HONORABLE

LADY ELEANOR BUTLER,

AND

MISS PONSONBY.

LUXURIANT Vale, thy Country's early boaft,
 What time great GLENDOUR gave thy fcenes to Fame;
Taught the proud numbers of the Englifh Hoft,
 How vain their vaunted force, when Freedom's flame
Fir'd him to brave the Myriads he abhorr'd,
Wing'd his unerring fhaft, and edg'd his victor fword.

Here firft thofe orbs unclofing drank the light,
 Cambria's bright ftars, the meteors of her Foes;
What dread and dubious omens* mark'd the night,
 That lour'd, ere yet his natal morn arofe!
The Steeds paternal, on their cavern'd floor,
Foaming, and horror-ftruck, " fret fetlock-deep in gore."

---

* *Omens.* According to the records of Lewis Owen, the year 1349 was dif-
tinguifhed by the firft appearance of the PESTILENCE in Wales, and by the birth
of OWEN GLENDOUR. Hollingfhed relates the marvellous tale of his Father's

B

PLAGUE, in her livid hand, o'er all the Ifle,

   Shook her dark flag, impure with fetid ftains;

While " DEATH*, on his pale Horfe," with baleful fmile,

   Smote with its blafting hoof the frighted plains.

Soon thro' the grafs-grown ftreets, in filence led,

Slow moves the midnight Cart, heapt with the naked Dead.

Yet in the feftal dawn of Richard's† reign,

   Thy gallant GLENDOUR's funny prime arofe;

Virtuous, tho' gay, in that Circean fane,

   Bright Science twin'd her circlet round his brows;

Nor cou'd the youthful, rafh, luxurious King

Diffolve the Hero's worth on his Icarian wing.

Sudden it drops on its meridian flight!——

   Ah! haplefs Richard! never didft thou aim

To crufh primeval Britons with thy might,

   And their brave Glendour's tears embalm thy name.

Back from thy victor-Rival's vaunting Throng,

Sorrowing, and ftern, he finks LLANGOLLEN's fhades among.

Horfes, being found that night in their ftables, ftanding up to the middle in blood.
The Bard, IOLO GOCH, mentions a Comet, which marked the great deeds of Glendour, when he was in the meridian of his glory. *See Mr.* PENNANT's TOUR.

      * Ifaiah.   † Richard the Second.

Soon, in imperious Henry's* dazzled eyes,
  The guardian bounds of juft Dominion melt;
His fcarce-hop'd crown imperfect blifs fupplies,
  Till Cambria's vaffalage be deeply felt.
Now up her craggy fteeps, in long array,
Swarm his exulting Bands, impatient for the fray.

Lo! thro' the gloomy night, with angry blaze,
  Trails the fierce Comet, and alarms the Stars;
Each waning Orb withdraws its glancing rays,
  Save the red Planet, that delights in wars.
Then, with broad eyes upturn'd, and ftarting hair,
Gaze the aftonifh'd Crowd upon its vengeful glare.

Gleams the wan Morn, and thro' LLANGOLLEN's Vale
  Sees the proud Armies ftreaming o'er her meads.
Her frighted Echos warning founds affail,
  Loud, in the rattling cars, the neighing fteeds;
The doubling drums, the trumpet's piercing breath,
And all the enfigns dread of havoc, wounds, and death.

---

* Henry the Fourth.

High on a hill as fhrinking CAMBRIA ftood,

   And watch'd the onfet of th' unequal fray,

She faw her Deva, ftain'd with warrior-blood,

   Lave the pale rocks, and wind its fateful way

Thro' meads, and glens, and wild woods, echoing far

The din of clafhing arms, and furious fhout of war.

From rock to rock, with loud acclaim, fhe fprung,

   While from her CHIEF the routed Legions fled;

Saw Deva roll their flaughter'd heaps among,

   The check'd waves eddying round the ghaftly dead ;

Saw, in that hour, her own LLANGOLLEN claim

Thermopylæ's bright wreath, and aye-enduring fame.

Thus, confecrate to GLORY.---Then arofe

   A milder luftre in its blooming maze ;

Thro' the green glens, where lucid Deva flows,

   Rapt Cambria liftens with enthufiaft gaze,

While more inchanting founds her ear affail,

Than thrill'd on Sorga's bank, the Love-devoted Vale.*

---

* *Vauclufe*, the celebrated Valley near Avignon, in which Petrarch compofed his beautiful Sonnets to Laura.

'Mid the gay towers on steep Din's* Branna's cone,

   Her HOEL's breast the fair MIFANWY fires.——

O! Harp of Cambria, never hast thou known

   Notes more mellifluent floating o'er the wires,

Than when thy Bard this brighter Laura sung,,

And with his ill-starr'd love LLANGOLLEN's echos rung.

Tho' Genius, Love, and Truth inspire the strains,

   Thro' Hoel's veins, tho' blood illustrious flows,

Hard as th' Eglwyseg rocks† her heart remains,

   Her smile a sun-beam playing on their snows ;

And nought avails the Poet's warbled claim,

But, by his well-sung woes, to purchase deathless fame.

---

* In 1390, Castel Dinas-Brân, now a bare ruin, was inhabited by the lovely Lady MIFANWY VECHAN, of the House of Tudor Trevor. She was beloved by the Bard HOEL. *See* MR. PENNANT's TOUR, adorned by a pleasing translation, in English verse, of one of Hoel's Poems in her praise, and complaining of her coldness. The ruins of Castel Dinas-Brân, are on a conoid mountain of laborious access. It rises in the midst of Llangollen Valley.

† *Eglwyseg rocks. Rocks of the Eagles.* They are opposite Castel Dinas-Brân. The Rev. Mr. Roberts of Dinbren asserts, that the word *Eglwyseg*, has that interpretation. Mr. PENNANT derives it from the name of a Gentleman, to whose memory the neighbouring column was erected; though, in another part of his Tour, he mentions Leland's testimony, that a pair of Eagles built annually in the Eglwyseg rocks, and that a person was let down in a basket to take the young, with another basket over his head, to protect him from the fury of the parent-birds. This tradition favors Mr. Roberts' etymology. That Gentleman has lately added largely to his paternal house, situated on a noble mountain in Llangollen Valley. The

Thus confecrate to Love, in ages flown,——

Long ages fled Din's-Branna's ruins fhow,

Bleak as they ftand upon their fteepy cone,

The crown and contraft of the VALE below,

That, fcreen'd by mural rocks, with pride difplays

Beauty's romantic pomp in every fylvan maze.

Now with a Veftal luftre glows the VALE,

Thine, facred FRIENDSHIP, permanent as pure;

In vain the ftern Authorities affail,

In vain Perfuafion fpreads her filken lure,

High-born, and high-endow'd, the peerlefs Twain*,

Pant for coy Nature's charms 'mid filent dale, and plain.

houfe ftands near its craggy fummit, and looks as if it had been fcooped out of the rocks. A very narrow Valley, containing two floping copfes, and a few bright little fields, with a woody lane winding between them, divides Mr. Roberts' mountain from the oppofite elevation of Caftel Dinas-Brân. The fouth-eaft front of the houfe looks immediately into this narrow Valley; the barren, and very fingular Eglwyfeg rocks on the left, and Caftel Dinas-Brân in front. Between the bafe of the latter, and the floping foot of his own mountain, Mr. R. has the bird's-eye profpeft of Llangollen Town, and a part of the Vale.—The Author of this Poem, is indebted to the friendly hofpitality of MR. and MRS. ROBERTS, for an opportunity (during a fortnight's refidence with them laft Summer) of contemplating the beauties of their own fcene, and of the celebrated VALLEY of LLANGOLLEN.

* *Peerlefs Twain.* RIGHT HONORABLE LADY ELEANOR BUTLER, and MISS PONSONBY, now feventeen years refident in Llangollen Vale, and whofe Gueft the Author had the honor to be during feveral delightful days of the late Summer.

Thro' ELEANORA, and her ZARA's mind,

    Early tho' genius, tafte, and fancy flow'd,

Tho' all the graceful Arts their powers combin'd,

    And her laft polifh brilliant Life beftow'd,

The lavifh Promifer, in Youth's foft morn, .   [fcorn.

Pride, Pomp, and Love, her friends, the fweet Enthufiafts

Then rofe the Fairy Palace of the Vale,

    Then bloom'd around it the Arcadian bowers;

Screen'd from the ftorms of Winter, cold and pale,

    Screen'd from the fervors of the fultry hours,

Circling the lawny crefcent, foon they rofe,

To letter'd eafe devote, and Friendfhip's bleft repofe.

Smiling they rofe beneath the plaftic hand

    Of Energy, and Tafte ;—nor only they,

Obedient Science hears the mild command,

    Brings every gift that fpeeds the tardy day,

Whate'er the pencil fheds in vivid hues,

Th' hiftoric tome reveals, or fings the raptur'd Mufe.

How ſweet to enter, at the twilight grey,

   The dear, minute Lyceum* of the Dome,

When, thro' the colour'd cryſtal, glares the ray,

   Sanguine and ſolemn 'mid the gathering gloom,

While glow-worm lamps diffuſe a pale, green light,

Such as in moſſy lanes illume the ſtarleſs night.

Then the coy Scene, by deep'ning veils o'erdrawn,

   In ſhadowy elegance ſeems lovelier ſtill;

Tall ſhrubs, that ſkirt the ſemi-lunar lawn,

   Dark woods, that curtain the oppoſing hill;

While o'er their brows the bare cliff faintly gleams,

And, from its paly edge, the evening-diamond† ſtreams.

* *Lyceum*,—the *Library*, fitted up in the Gothic taſte, the painted windows of that form. In the elliptic arch of the door, there is a priſmatic lantern of variouſly tinted glaſs, containing two large lamps with their reflectors. The light they ſhed reſembles that of a Volcano, gloomily glaring. Oppoſite, on the chimney-piece, a couple of ſmall lamps, in marble reſervoirs, aſſiſt the priſmatic lantern to ſupply the place of candles, by a light more conſonant to the ſtyle of the apartment, the pictures it contains of abſent Friends, and to its aërial muſic.

† Evening-Star.

What ftrains Æolian thrill the dufk expanfe,

   As rifing gales with gentle murmurs play,

Wake the loud chords, or every fenfe intrance,

   While in fubfiding winds they fink away !

Like diftant choirs, " when pealing organs blow,"

And melting voices blend, majeftically flow.

" *But, ah ! what hand can touch the ftrings fo fine,

   " Who up the lofty diapafon roll

" Such fweet, fuch fad, fuch folemn airs divine,

   " Then let them down again into the foul !"

The prouder fex as foon, with virtue calm,   [palm.

Might win from this bright Pair pure Friendfhip's fpotlefs

What boafts Tradition, what th' hiftoric Theme,

   Stands it in all their chronicles confeft

Where the foul's glory fhines with clearer beam,

   Than in our fea-zon'd bulwark of the Weft,

When, in this Cambrian Valley, Virtue fhows

Where, in her own foft fex, its fteadieft luftre glows ?

* Thefe lines with inverted commas, are from Thomfon's *Caftle of Indolence.*

Say ivied VALLE CRUCIS*, time decay'd,

   Dim on the brink of Deva's wandering floods,

Your riv'd arch glimmering thro' the tangled glade,

   Your grey hills towering o'er your night of woods,

Deep in the Vale's receffes as you ftand,

And, defolately great, the rifing figh command,

Say, lonely, ruin'd Pile, when former years

   Saw your pale Train at midnight altars bow ;

Saw SUPERSTITION frown upon the tears

   That mourn'd the rafh irrevocable vow,

Wore one young lip gay ELEANORA's fmile?

Did ZARA's look ferene one tedious hour beguile ?

For your fad Sons, nor Science wak'd her powers;

   Nor e'er did Art her lively fpells difplay;

But the grim IDOL† vainly lafh'd the hours

   That dragg'd the mute, and melancholy day ;

Dropt her dark cowl on each devoted head,

That o'er the breathing Corfe a pall eternal fpread.

---

* The picturefque Ruins of *Valle Crucis* Abbey, one of the moft ftriking objects in this Valley. They are particularly defcribed by Mr. PENNANT, and there are engravings of them in his Tour.

† Superftition.

This gentle Pair no glooms of thought infeſt,
   Nor Bigotry, nor Envy's ſullen gleam
Shed withering influence on the effort bleſt,
   Which moſt ſhou'd win the other's dear eſteem,
By added knowledge, by endowment high,
By Charity's warm boon, and Pity's ſoothing ſigh.

Then how ſhou'd Summer-day or Winter-night,
   Seem long to them who thus can wing their hours!
O! ne'er may Pain, or Sorrow's cruel blight,
   Breathe the dark mildew thro' theſe lovely bowers,
But lengthen'd Life ſubſide in ſoft decay,
Illum'd by riſing Hope, and Faith's pervading ray.

May one kind ice-bolt, from the mortal ſtores,
   Arreſt each vital current as it flows,
That no ſad courſe of deſolated hours
   Here vainly nurſe the unſubſiding woes!
While all who honor Virtue, gently mourn
LLANGOLLEN'S VANISH'D PAIR, and wreath their ſacred urn.

VERSES

ON

WREXHAM,

AND THE

INHABITANTS OF ITS ENVIRONS.

PROUD of her ancient Race, Britannia fhows
Where, in her Wales, another Eden glows,
And all her Sons, to Truth, and Honor dear,
Prove they deferve the Paradife they fhare.

Thrice happy Wrexham, 'mid thy neighbouring groves
Stray, with 'twin'd arms, the Virtues, and the Loves,
There FLETCHER*, from her own Gwernheyled, beams,
Fair as its meads, and liberal as its ftreams ;
The Sifter APPERLYS†, in Youth's foft morn,
With rifing charms the feftal fcenes adorn ;
And friendly PRICE ‡, as happy, free, and gay,
As when, in Life and Beauty's rofy May,

---

* Mrs. Fletcher of *Gwernheyled*—Gwernheyled, means *Sunny Alders.*
† The two Mifs Apperlys.
‡ Mrs. Parry Price, late of that neighbourhood.

She fhone, the Hebe of her green retreat,
With half the youth of Cambria at her feet.
See CUNLIFFE's* eyes diffufe the gladdening ray,
And fhed around her Pleafure's golden day ;
Meridian lovelinefs, majeftic grace,
Stream o'er her form, and lighten in her face ;
While Senfe and Virtue's blended influence dart
The look, the voice, refiftlefs to the heart.

Nor only, WREXHAM, do thy circling groves
Boaft the fair Virtues, and the radiant Loves,
There HAYMAN's† fong, with its inchanting powers,
Floats thro' thy vales, thy manfions, and thy bowers ;
Her hallow'd temple there Religion fhows,
That erft with beauteous majefty arofe
In ancient days, when Gothic Art difplay'd
Her fanes, in airy elegance array'd,
Whofe namelefs charms the Dorian claims efface,
Corinthian fplendor, and Ionic grace ;
Then plied, with curious fkill, now rarely fhown,
Th' adorning chifel, o'er the yielding ftone.

* The Lady of Sir Fofter Cunliffe, Baronet.
† Watkin Hayman, Efq.

But as thofe Graces which alone delight
With their fine forms the captivated *fight*,
Muft not afpire to emulate the Art
That, while it charms the eye, pervades the *heart*,
See Gothic Elegance the palm refigns,
When Art in *intellectual* greatnefs fhines.
Bright as in *Albion's long diftinguifh'd fanes,
Within thefe holy Walls, fhe lives, fhe reigns.
Her SAINTED MAID†, amid the burfting tomb,
Hears the LAST TRUMPET thrill its murky gloom,
With fmile triumphant over DEATH, and Time,
Lifts the rapt eye, and rears the form fublime.

WREXHAM, for thee thus rofe, by mental power,
Fair modern Science o'er the Arts of yore;
For thee exulting fhe entwines the wreaths,
As SCULPTURE fpeaks, and heavenly MUSIC breathes,
Since great ROUBILLIAC decks thy SACRED SHRINE,
And GENIUS wakes thy RANDAL's HARP‡ divine.

* Weftminfter.

† *Sainted Maid.* Mrs. Mary Middleton's monument by Roubilliac, in the Chancel at Wrexham.

‡ Mr. *Randal,* Organift of Wrexham; an exquifite Performer on the pedal Harp. He has been blind from his infancy.

HOYLE LAKE*,

A

POEM,

WRITTEN ON THAT COAST,

AND ADDRESSED TO ITS PROPRIETOR,

SIR JOHN STANLEY.

THEE, STANLEY, thee, our gladden'd fpirit hails,
 Since Life's firft good for us thy efforts gain,
Who, Habitants of Albion's inland vales,
 Refide far diftant from her circling main.

Thefe lightfome Walls, beneath thy generous cares
 Arofe, the lawny fcene's convivial boaft,
While at thy voice clear-cheek'd Hygeia rears
 Her aqueous altars on this tepid coaft.

* *Hoyle Lake,* the real name, better fuited to verfe than its recently-affumed appellation, *High Lake.*

This coaſt, the neareſt to our central home,
    That green Britannia's watry zone diſplays,
Now gives the drooping Frame a cheerful Dome*,
    Whoſe Lares† ſmile, and promiſe lengthen'd days.

When gather'd fogs the pale horizon ſteep,
    Falling in heavy, deep, continual rain,
If, ere the Sun ſink ſhrouded in the deep,
    His cryſtal rays pervade the vapory train,

Dry are the turfy downs, diffuſive ſpread
    O'er the light ſurface of the ſandy mound,
Where e'en the languid Form may ſafely tread,
    Drink the pure gale, and eye the blue profound.

---

* The large and handſome Hotel, built in the year 1792, by SIR JOHN STAN-
LEY, and which converts theſe pleaſant Downs into a commodious ſea-bathing
Place.

† *Lares*, Houſehold-Gods.

Dear Scene !——that ftretch'd between the filver arms

    Of Deva*, and of Merfey, meets the main,

And when the fun-gilt day illumes its charms,

    Boafts of peculiar grace, nor boafts in vain.

Tho' near the Beach, dark Helbrie's lonely Ifle,

    Repofes fullen in the watry way,

Hears round her rocks the tides, returning, boil,

    And o'er her dufky fandals dafh their fpray.

Mark, to the left, romantic Cambria's coaft,

    Her curtain'd mountains rifing o'er the floods ;

While feas on Orm's beak'd promontory burft,

    Blue Deva fwells her mirror to the woods.

---

* *Deva*, the claffical name of the DEE.

    " Nor yet where Deva fpreads her wizard ftream."

                                 MILTON's Lycidas.

Alfo Prior, in Henry and Emma.

    " Him, great in peace and wealth, fair Deva knows."

MILTON, probably ufes the epithet *wifard*, in allufion to the rites and myfteries performed on the banks of the Deva, or Dee. In Spencer, that River is made the haunt of Magicians. That fine poetic Scholar and Critic, the late Mr. T. WARTON, obferves, in his Edition of Milton's leffer Poems, that MERLIN ufed to vifit old Timon in a green Valley, at the foot of the Mountain, Rauran-Vaur, in Merionethfhire, from which Mountain the River Deva fprings. *See Fairy Queen,* B. 1. C. ix. V. 4. In Drayton, an old Poet, with whofe works Milton was familiar, it is ftyled " the *hallowed,* the *holy,* the *ominous flood.*"

High o'er that varied ridge of Alpine forms,
    Vaſt MOEL-Y-FAMMAU* towers upon the ſight,
Lifts her maternal boſom to the ſtorms,
    And ſcreens her filial mountains from their blight.

Far on the right, the dim Lancaſtrian plains,
    In pallid diſtance, glimmer thro' the ſky,
Tho', hid by jutting rocks, thy ſplendid fanes,
    Commercial Liverpool, elude the eye.

Wide in the front the confluent Oceans roll,
    Amid whoſe reſtleſs billows guardian Hoyle,
To ſcreen her azure Lake when Tempeſts howl,
    Spreads the firm texture of her amber Iſle†.

And tho' the ſurging Tide's reſiſtleſs waves
    Roll, day, and night, its level ſurface o'er,
Tho' the ſkies darken, and the whirlwind raves,
    They froth,—but ruſh innoxious to the ſhore.

---

* *Moel-y-Fammau*, the firſt word ſpoken as one ſyllable, as if ſpelt *Mole*. The name ſignifies in Welch, *Mother of Mountains*. It is ſeen in the Hoyle-Lake proſpect, behind the Flintſhire Hills, and conſiderably higher than any of them.

† *Amber Iſle*, the *Sand Iſland*, ſix miles long, and four broad, which lying in the Sea, a mile from ſhore, forms the Lake; and breaking the force of the Tides, conſtitutes the ſafety of that Lake as an Harbour and Bathing-Place.

When fear-ftruck fea-men, 'mid the raging flood,
   Hear thundering SHIPWRECK yell her dire decrees,
See her pale arm rend every fail, and fhroud,
   And o'er the high maft lift her whelming feas,

If to thy quiet harbour, gentle Hoyle,
   The fhatter'd Navy thro' the tempeft flies,
Each joyous Mariner forgets his toil,
   And carols to the vainly angry fkies.

What tho' they vex the Lake's cerulean ftream,
   And curl its billows on the fhelly floor,
Yet, in defpite of Fancy's timid dream,
   Age, and Infirmity, may plunge fecure.

How gay the Scene when Spring's fair mornings break,
   Or Summer-noons illume the graffy mound,
When anchor'd Navies crowd the peopled Lake,
   Or deck the diftant Ocean's fkiey bound.

Like leaflefs forefts, on its verge extreme
   Rife the tall mafts;—or fpreading wide their fails,
Silvering, and fhining in the folar beam,
   Stand on that laft blue line, and court the gales.

The peopled Lake, of fong, and lively cheer,

    And Boatfwain's whiftle bears the jovial found;

While rofy pennants, floating on the air,

    Tinge the foft feas of glafs, that fleep around.

'Twas on thefe Downs * the Belgian Hero fpread

    His ardent Legions in aufpicious hours,

Ere to Ierne's hoftile fhores he led

    To deathlefs glory their embattled Powers.

When, like the Conqueror of the Eaftern World,

    That ftemm'd with dauntlefs breaft the Granic flood,

His victor-fword immortal WILLIAM whirl'd,

    And Boyne's pale waters dyed with Rebel blood.

Since now, to health devoted, this calm fhore

    Breathes renovation in its foamy wave,

For the kind DONOR fhall each heart implore,

    The good his energies to others gave.

---

  * KING WILLIAM encamped his army on the Hoyle Lake Downs, before he took fhipping from thence, on his victorious expedition to Ireland.

That long on him clear-cheek'd Hygeia's ſmile,
   And long on all he loves, ſerene may ſhine,
Who from thy ſparkling coaſt, benignant HOYLE,
   Diffus'd the bleſſings of her cryſtal ſhrine.

HERVA*,

AT THE TOMB OF
ARGANTYR.

A

RUNIC DIALOGUE.

HERVA.

ARGANTYR, wake!—to thee I call,
Hear from thy dark fepulchral hall !
'Mid the Foreft's inmoft gloom,
Thy Daughter, circling thrice thy tomb,

Hervor. " Awake, Argantyr!—Hervor, the Daughter of thee and Sauferlama,
" doth awaken thee! Give me out of the tomb the hardened fword which the
" Dwarfs made for Sauferlama."

---

* Doftor Hicks' literal profe Tranflation in his *Thefaurus Septentrionalis,* of this
ancient Norfe Poem, is here given to gratify the reader's curiofity; alfo to fhow that
it is ufed only as an outline, and that the following Poem is a bold Paraphrafe, not
a Tranflation. The expreffions in Dr. Hicks' profe, have a vulgar familiarity, in-
jurious to the fublimity of the original conception. A clofe tranflation, in Englifh
verfe, will be found in a valuable colleftion of Runic Odes, by the ingenious and
learned Mr. Mathias. After his example, fome flight changes have been made in
the names, for their better accommodation to the verfe.

With myſtic rites of thrilling power
Diſturbs thee at this midnight hour !
I, thy Sauferlama's child,
Of my filial right beguil'd,
Now adjure thee to reſign
The CHARMED SWORD, by birth-right mine !
When the Dwarf, on Eyvor's plain,
Dim glided by thy marriage-train,
In jewel'd belt of gorgeous pride,
To thy pale and trembling Bride,
Gave he not, in whiſper deep,
That dread companion of thy ſleep ?—
Fall'n before its edge thy foes,
Idly does it now repoſe
In the dark tomb with thee?—awake !
Spells thy ſullen ſlumber break !
Now their ſtern command fulfill !—
Warrior, art thou ſilent ſtill?—
Or are my groſs ſenſes found
Deaf to the low ſepulchral ſound?—

HERVARDOR,—HIARVARDOR,—hear!

HRANI, mid thy flumber drear!

Spirits of a dauntlefs Race,

In armor clad, your tombs I trace.

Now, with fharp and blood-ftain'd fpear,

Accent fhrill, and fpell fevere,

I wake you all from flumber mute,

Beneath the dark Oak's twifted root!—

Are Andgrym's hated Sons no more

That fleeps the SWORD, that drank their gore?—

Living,—why, to MAGIC RHYME,

Speaks no voice of former time,

Low as o'er your tombs I bend

To hear th' expected founds afcend,

Murmuring from your darkfome hall,

At a Virgin's folemn call?—

" Hervardur, Hiarvardur, Hrani,—with helmet and coat of mail, and a fharp fword,
  " with fhield and accoutrements, and a bloody fpear, I awaken vou all under
  " the roots of Trees.

" Are the Sons of Andgrym, who delighted in mifchief, now become duft and
  " afhes?—Can none of Eyvor's Sons fpeak to me out of the habitations of
  " the dead?"—

HERVARDOR,——HIARVARDOR,——hear !

HRANI,——mark my spell severe!

Henceforth may the semblance* cold,

That did each Warrior's spirit hold,

Parch, as Corse unblest, that lies

Withering in the sultry skies !——

Ghastly may your forms decay,

Hence the noisome reptile's prey,

If ye force not, thus adjur'd,

My Sire to yield the CHARMED SWORD!

" Hervardur, Hiarvardur, Hrani!—so may you all be within your ribs, as a thing " that is hanged up to putrify among insects, unless you cause Argantyr to " deliver up to me the *sword* which the Dwarfs made, and the glorious belt!"

* According to the Gothic Mythology, the spirits of Heros slept in their bodies, which did not decay. Putrefaction, therefore, was the heaviest curse that could be denounced.

" Never shall Enquirer come
" To break my iron-sleep again,
" Till Lok has burst his ten-fold chain."

GRAY's Descent of Odin, from the
Norse Poetry.

E

ARGANTYR.

Arm'd amid this ftarlefs gloom,
Thou, whofe fteps adventurous roam;
Thou, that wav'ft a magic fpear
Thrice before our manfions drear,
Devoted Virgin,—know in time
The mifchiefs of the RUNIC RHYME,
Forcing accents, mutter'd deep,
From the cold reluctant lip!
Me no tender Father laid
Entomb'd beneath an hallow'd fhade;
It was no friendly voice that gave
The Oak, that fcreen'd a Warrior's grave,
Gave it, in malignant tone,
To the blafting thunderftone.—
Timelefs now thefe bones decay,
Pervious to the baleful ray

" *Argantyr.* Daughter Hervor, full of fpells to raife the dead, why doft thou
" call fo?—wilt thou run on to thine own mifchief?—Thou art mad, and out
" of thy fenfes, who art defperately refolved to awaken dead men!"—

" I was not buried either by Father or other Friends—Two which lived after me,
" got *Turfing*, one of whom is now poffeffor thereof."

Of the fwart ftar.—'Mid Battle's yell
The charm'd, the fatal Weapon fell
From my unwary grafp.—A Knight
Seiz'd the Sword of magic might.
Virgin, of thy fpells demand
His name,—and from his victor hand,
Try if thy intrepid zeal
May win the all-fubduing Steel.

HERVA.

Warrior,—thus, with falfehood wild,
Seek'ft thou to deceive thy child?—
Sure as Odin doom'd thy fall,
And hides thee in this filent hall,
Here fleeps the Sword.—Pale Chief, refign
That, which is by birthright mine!
Fear'ft thou, Spirit of my Sire,
At thy only Child's defire,
Glorious heritage to yield,
Conqueft in the deathful field?

" *Hervor.* Thou doft not tell the truth—fo let Odin hide thee in the tomb, as
" thou haft got *Turfing* by thee. Art thou unwilling, *Argantyr*, to give an
" inheritance to thy only child?"—

ARGANTYR.

Daring HERVA, liften yet,
Spare thy heart its long regret!
Why trembling fhrunk thy Mother's frame
When the FATAL PRESENT came?
Virgin, mark the boding word,
Sullen whifper'd o'er the SWORD!
It prophecied Argantyr's Foes
Shou'd rue its prowefs;—yet that woes
Greater far his RACE fhou'd feel,
Victims of the CRUEL STEEL,
When, in blood of millions dyed,
It arms an ireful Fratricide.
　MAID, no erring accents warn;——
Of Sons to thee, hereafter born,
One thy Chiefs fhall HYDRECK name,
Dark fpirited!—but dear to fame
Shall blooming HIARALMO live.——
Maid, his doom thy mandates give!

" *Argantyr.* I will tell thee, Hervor, what is to come to. pafs.—This *Turfing*
" will, if thou doft believe me, deftroy almoft all thy offspring.—Thou fhalt
" have a Son, and many think that he will be called *Hydrec* by the People."

Renounce, renounce the dire demand,

Or to thy Sons, in HYDRECK's hand,

Fatal proves, fome future day,

The CHARMED SWORD.—Difturb it not!—away!

HERVA.

ARGANTYR,—hear thy Daughter's voice,

Spells decree an only choice!

Or, in perturbed tomb unbleft,

The filence of fepulchral reft

Shall no more thy funk eye fteep,

Clofe no more thy pallid lip,

Or, ere this night's fhadows melt,

Mine the SWORD, and gorgeous belt.

ARGANTYR.

Young Maid,—who as of warrior might,

Roameft thus to tombs by night,

In coat of mail, with voice auftere,

Waving the Corfe-awakening SPEAR

O'er thy dead Anceftors;—offence,

And danger threaten!—hie thee hence!

" *Hervor.* I do, by Enchantments, make that the Dead fhall never know peace, or
" reft, unlefs thou deliver up to me *Turfing.*"

" *Argantyr.* Young Maid, I fay thou art of manlike courage, who doft roam
" about by night to tombs, with fpear engraven by magical fpells, with hel-
" met and coat of mail, before the door of our Hall."

HERVA.

Obey, obey, or fleep no more!

Now my facred right reftore!

The SWORD, that joys when Foes affail,

Sword, that fcorns the ribbed mail,

Scorns the car, in fwift career,

Scorns the helmet, fcorns the fpear;

Scorns the nerv'd experienc'd arm;

ARGANTYR, yield it to my charm!

'Tis not well the Victor's pride,

With thee in filent tombs to hide;

Thy Child, thy only Child, demands,—

Reach it with thy wither'd hands!

ARGANTYR.

The death of HIARALMO lies

Beneath this mouldering arm!—and rife

Round its edge, the lurid fires,

Hoftile to unaw'd defires.

Hie thee hence, nor madly dare

The death-denouncing grafp;—beware!

" *Hervor.* I took thee for a brave man before I found out your halls. Give me
" out of the tomb the workmanfhip of the *Dwarfs*, which hates all coats of
" mail.—It is not good for thee to hide it."

" *Argantyr.* The death of *Hialmor* lies beneath my fhoulders.—It is all wrapt
" up in fire. I know no Maid of any Country that dares take this *Sword* in
" hand."

HERVA.

Not if thoufand fires invade
Streaming from its angry blade.
Innoxious are the fires that play
Round the Corfe, with meteor ray,
And in thefe wafte hours of night
Silent death-halls dimly light;
Yet, gliding with confuming force,
Undaunted wou'd I meet their courfe.

ARGANTYR.

Thou, whofe awlefs voice proclaims
Scorn of the fepulchral flames,
Left their force around thee fwell,
Punifhing thy daring fpell,
And thy mortal form confume,
HERVA, fee!—thy Father's tomb

" *Hervor.* I fhall take and keep it in my hand, if I may obtain it.—I do not
" think the fires will burn that play about the fight of deceafed men."

" *Argantyr.* O, conceited *Hervor,* thou art mad! Rather than thou fhouldeft
" in an inflant fall into the fire, I will give thee the *Sword,* O, young Maid,
" and not hide it from thee."

Opens!—mark, to thee reftor'd,

Rifing flow, the baneful Sword!—

See, it meets thy rafh defire

*Bickering with funereal fire !

Herva.

Warrior, now doft thou reclaim

The luftre of thy former fame;

Lo, the Sword, a feeming brand,

Blazes in thy Daughter's hand!

Nor perifhes that hand beneath

Vaporous flames, that round it wreathe,

Gleam along the midnight air,

Illume the foreft wide,—and glare

On the fcath'd Oak !—Sepulchral wood,

Thee I quit for fields of blood !

Nor would I, on its fateful range,

This Sword, with all its meteors, change

For the Norweyan fceptre.—Lo,

Death, and conqueft, wait me now !—

" *Hervor.* Thou doft well, Offspring of Heroes, that thou doft give me the
" *Sword* out of the Tomb.—I am now better pleafed, O Prince, to have it,
" than if I had got all Norway."

* " And from about him fierce effufion roll'd
" Of fmoke, and *bickering flame,* and fparkles dire."

Milton's Par. Loft. B. vi. line 765.

ARGANTYR.

HIARALMO's future bane,

Grafp'd with exultation vain,

Fatal, fatal fhall be found

To thee, and thine, in curelefs wound!

By that wound 'tis now decreed

HYDREK's felf at length fhall bleed!

Herva, lefs thy long regret

Had thy Chiefs in combat met

Andgrym's fons, with warlike zeal,

Met them in *uncharmed* fteel.

HERVA.

Sleep, Argantyr,—Chief of might,

Thro' the long, the dreary night;

Nor let ftrife, and bitter fcorn,

'Mid Herva's offspring, yet unborn,

" *Argantyr.* Falfe Woman!—thou doft not underftand that thou fpeakeft
" foolifhly of that in which thou doft rejoice.—*Turfing* fhall, if thou wilt be-
" lieve me, deftroy all thy offspring."

" *Hervor.* I muft go to my Seamen,—here I have no mind to ftay any longer.—
" Little do I care, O royal Friend, what my Sons hereafter quarrel about."

F

Difturb thee in the tomb !—and mark,
The Spear, that broke thy flumber dark,
Round the blafted Oak I wave,
That ill protects a Warrior's grave !
Soon fhall its fcath'd trunk be feen
Cloth'd in fhielding bark, and green
As before the vengeful time,
When, by force of baleful Rhyme,
It fhrunk amid the foreft's groan,
Smote by the red thunderftone.
Thro' the renovated boughs,
Guardians of thy deep repofe,
Shall the hail no longer pour,
The livid Dog-ftar look no more !
Spirits of the elder Dead,
Spell-awak'd from flumber dread,
Not to your fpears, in martial pride,
Refting by each Hero's fide,
Not to your gore-fpotted mail,
Steely fhroud of Warrior pale,
Shall, thro' thoufand Winters, drain
Driving fnow, or drenching rain;
Nor, while countlefs Summers beam
On arid plain, or fhrinking ftream,

Thro' the widening chink be known

Reptile vile of fultry Noon,

To wind the flimy track abhorr'd!—

Fate is mine, fince mine the SWORD!

ARGANTYR.

Herva, thine the fource of woes,

Direful long to all thy foes,

Ere againft thy peace it turn,

And thou thy bleeding Race fhalt mourn.

When extinct the tomb's blue fires,

Whofe light now gleams, and now retires,

Quivering o'er its edge, forbear

To touch the VENOM'D BLADE ;—beware !

Venom, for the blood prepar'd

Of twelve brave Chiefs, their dread reward.

" *Argantyr.* Take and keep Hialmor's bane, which thou fhalt long have and
  " enjoy.—Touch not the edges, there is poifon on both of them!—It is a
  " moft cruel Devourer of Men!"

" Farewell Daughter.—I do quickly give thee the twelve men's deaths, if thou
  " canft believe with might and courage,—and all the goods that Andgrym's
  " Sons have left behind them."

Herva, now thy Father's tomb
Slowly clofes !—Ne'er prefume
Again to breathe, in Odin's hall,
Shrill, the Corfe-difturbing call!

HERVA.

I go,—for thefe blue fires infeft
The troubled tomb's prefumptuous Gueft ;
As of ftep profane aware,
Round me, more and more, they glare.—
Hervardor, Hiarvardor,—keep
Lafting flumber!—Hrani fleep!
And fleep ARGANTYR!—Chiefs of might,
Quiet be your mornlefs night!

" *Hervor.* Dwell, all of you fafe in the Tombs! I muft be gone and haften
" hence, for I feem to be in a place where fire burns about me."

EYAM*.

FOR one fhort week I leave, with anxious heart,
Source of my filial cares, the FULL OF DAYS;
Lur'd by the promife of harmonic Art
To breathe her Handel's foul-exalting lays.
Penfive I trace the Derwent's amber wave†,
Foaming thro' fylvan banks, or view it lave
The foft romantic vallies, high o'er-peer'd
By hills, and rocks, in favage grandeur rear'd.

Not two fhort miles from thee,—can I refrain
Thy haunts, my native EYAM, long unfeen?
Thou, and thy lov'd Inhabitants again
Shall meet my tranfient gaze,—Thy rocky fcreen,

---

* This Poem was written Auguft 1788, on a journey through Derbyfhire, to
a mufic-meeting at Sheffield. The Author's Father was Rector of EYAM, an ex-
tenfive Village, that runs along a mountainous terrace, in one of the higheft parts
of the Peak. She was born there, and there paffed the firft feven years of her
life, vifiting the Place often with her Father in future periods. The middle part of
this Village is built on the edge of a deep Dell, which has very picturefque, and
beautiful features.

† *Amber wave.* From the peculiar nature of the clay on the mountains, from
which it defcends, the River Derwent has a yellow tint, that well becomes the dark
foliage on its banks, and the perpetual foam produced by a narrow, and rocky
·channel.

Thy airy cliffs I mount; and feek thy fhade,
Thy roofs, that brow the fteep, romantic glade;
But, while on me the eyes of Friendfhip glow,
Swell my pain'd fighs, my tears fpontaneous flow.

In Scenes paternal, not beheld thro' years,
Nor view'd, till *now*, but by a Father's fide,
Well might the tender tributary tears,
From keen regrets of duteous fondnefs, glide.
Its Paftor, to this Human-Flock no more
Shall the long flight of future days reftore;
Diftant he droops——and that once-gladdening eye
Now languid gleams, e'en when his Friends are nigh.

Thro' this known walk, where weedy gravel lies,
Rough, and unfightly;—by the long coarfe grafs
Of the once fmooth, and vivid Green, with fighs,
To the deferted Rectory I pafs;—
Stray thro' the darken'd chambers naked bound,
Where Childhood's earlieft, livelieft blifs I found.
How chang'd, fince erft, the lightfome walls beneath,
The focial joys did their warm comforts breathe!

Ere yet I go, who may return no more, .
That facred Pile, 'mid yonder fhadowy trees,
Let me revifit!—ancient, maffy door,
Thou grateft hoarfe!—my vital fpirits freeze
Paffing the vacant Pulpit to the fpace
Where humble rails the decent Altar grace,
And where my infant fifter's afhes fleep,
Whofe lofs I left the childifh fport to weep.

*Now the low beams, with paper garlands hung,
In memory of fome village Youth, or Maid,
Draw the foft tear, from thrill'd remembrance fprung,
How oft my childhood mark'd that tribute paid.
The gloves fufpended by the garland's fide,
White as its fnowy flowers, with ribbands tied;
Dear Village! long thefe wreaths funereal fpread,
Simple memorials of thy early Dead !

---

* The ancient cuftom of hanging a garland of white rofes, made of writing-
paper, and a pair of white gloves, over the pew of the unmarried Villagers, who
die in the flower of their age, is obferved to this day, in the Village of EYAM, and
in moft other Villages, and little Towns in the Peak.

But, O! thou blank, and filent Pulpit!—thou
That with a Father's precepts, juft, and bland,
Did'ft win my ear, as Reafon's ftrengthening glow
Show'd their full value—now thou feem'ft to ftand
Before my fad, fuffus'd, and trembling gaze,
The drearieft relic of departed days ;
Of eloquence paternal, nervous, clear,
DIM APPARITION THOU,—and bitter is my tear.

TO

TIME PAST.

WRITTEN DEC. 1772.

RETURN, bleft years!— when not the jocund Spring,
Luxuriant Summer, nor the amber hours
Calm Autumn gives, my heart invok'd to bring
Joys, whofe rich balm o'er all the bofom pours;
When ne'er I wifh'd might grace the clofing day
One tint purpureal, or one golden ray;
When the loud Storms, that defolate the bowers,
Found dearer welcome than Favonian gales,   [Vales!
And Winter's bare, bleak fields, than Summer's flowery

Yet, not to deck pale hours with vain parade
Beneath the blaze of wide-illumin'd Dome;
Not for the bounding Dance;—not to pervade,
And charm the fenfe with Mufic;—nor, as roam
The mimic Paffions o'er theatric fcene,
To laugh, or weep;—O! not for thefe, I ween,
But for delights that made the *heart* their home,
Was the grey night-froft on the founding plain
More than the Sun invok'd, that gilds the graffy lane.

G

Yes, for the joys that trivial joys excell,

My lov'd HONORA*, did we hail the gloom

Of dim November's eve;—and as it fell,

And the bright fires fhone cheerful round the room,

Dropt the warm curtains with no tardy hand ;

And felt our fpirits, and our hearts expand,

Liftening their fteps, who ftill, where'er they come,

Make the keen ftars, that glaze the fettled fnows,

More than the Sun invok'd, when firft he tints the rofe.

Affection,—Friendfhip,—Sympathy,—your throne

Is Winter's glowing hearth;—and ye were ours,

Thy fmile, HONORA, made them all our own.—

Where are they *now?*—alas! their choiceft powers

Faded at thy retreat ;—for thou art gone,

And many a dark, long Eve I figh alone,

In thrill'd remembrance of the vanifh'd hours,

When ftorms were dearer than the balmy gales,

And Winter's bare bleak fields than green luxuriant vales.

---

* MISS HONORA SNEYD, to whom the gallant, and unfortunate MAJOR ANDRE, was fo unalienably attached. See the Author's MONODY on that Gentleman.

The following are felected from a centenary of SONNETS, written as occafion prefented the Idea, through a Courfe of more than twenty Years. The Author intends to publifh them collectively at fome future period.

SONNET.

INGRATITUDE,—how deadly is thy fmart,
　　Proceeding from the Form we fondly love !
　　How light, compar'd, all other forrows prove!
　　Thou fhed'ft a night of woe, from whence depart
The gentle beams of patience, that the heart
　　'Mid leffer ills illume.—Thy Victims rove
　　Unquiet as the Ghoft that haunts the grove
　　Where MURDER fpilt the life-blood.—O! thy dart
Kills more than life, e'en all that makes it dear;
　　Till we the " fenfible of pain" wou'd change
　　For Phrenzy, that defies the bitter tear,
Or wifh, in kindred calloufnefs, to range
　　Where moon-ey'd IDIOCY, with fallen lip,
　　Drags the loofe knee, and intermitting ftep.

SONNET,

WRITTEN ON RISING GROUND,

NEAR LICHFIELD.

The Evening ſhines in May's luxuriant pride,
 And all the ſunny hills at diſtance glow,
 And all the brooks that thro' the Valley flow,
 Seem liquid gold.—O! had my fate denied
Leiſure, and power to taſte the ſweets, that glide
 Thro' kindling Souls, as the ſoft Seaſons go
 On their ſtill varying progreſs, for the woe
 My heart has felt, what balm had been ſupplied?—
But where great NATURE ſmiles, as *here* ſhe ſmiles,
 'Mid verdant vales, and gently-ſwelling hills,
 And glaſſy lakes, and mazy, murmuring rills,
And narrow wood-wild lanes, her ſpell beguiles
 Th' impatient ſighs of grief, and reconciles
 Poetic minds to Life, with all her ills.

SONNET,

TO A

YOUNG LADY IN AFFLICTION,

WHO THOUGHT SHE SHOULD NEVER MORE BE HAPPY;

WRITTEN ON THE SEA-SHORE.

Yes, thou ſhalt ſmile again!—Time always heals,
  In Youth, the wounds of ſorrow.—O! ſurvey
  Yon now ſubſided Deep, thro' night a prey
  To warring winds, and to their furious peals
Surging tumultuous.—Yet, as in diſmay,
  The ſettling billows tremble—Morning ſteals
  Grey on the rocks; and ſoon, to pour the day
  From the ſtreak'd eaſt, the radiant Orb unveils,
In all his pride of light.—Thus ſhall the glow
  Of beauty, health, and hope, by ſoft degrees
  Spread o'er thy breaſt ;—diſperſe theſe ſtorms of woe:
Wake with ſoft Pleaſure's ſenſe, the wiſh to pleaſe,
  Till from thoſe eyes the wonted luſtres flow,
  Bright as the Sun, on calm, and cryſtal Seas.

SONNET.

Now, young-ey'd Spring, on gentle breezes borne,
    'Mid the deep woodlands, hills, and vales, and bowers,
    Unfolds her leaves, her bloſſoms, and her flowers,
    Pouring their ſoft luxuriance on the morn.
O! how unlike the wither'd, wan, and worn,
    And limping Winter, that o'er ruſſet moors,
    And plaſhy fields, and ice-incruſted ſhores
    Strays,—and commands his riſing winds to mourn!
Protraƈted Life, thou art ordain'd to wear
    A form like his;—and, ſhou'd thy gifts be mine,
    I tremble leſt a kindred influence drear
Steal on my mind;—but pious Hope benign,
    The Soul's new day-ſpring, ſhall avert the fear,
    And gild Exiſtence in her dim decline.

SONNET.

INVITATION TO A FRIEND.

Since dark December fhrouds the tranfient day,
    And ftormy Winds are howling in their ire,
    Why com'ft not THOU, who always can'ft infpire
    The foul of cheerfulnefs, and beft array
A fullen hour in fmiles?—O ! hafte to pay
    The cordial vifit fullen hours require !
    Around the circling Walls a glowing fire
    Shines ;—but it vainly fhines in this delay
To blend thy fpirit's warm Promethean light.
    Come then, at Science, and at Friendfhip's call,
    Their vow'd Difciple;—come, for they invite ;
The focial Powers without thee languifh all.
Come,—that I may not *hear* the winds of night,
    Nor *count* the heavy eve-drops as they fall !

SONNET.

If he whofe bofom with no tranfport fwells
    In vernal airs, and hours, commits the crime
    Of fullennefs to Nature; 'gainft the time,
    And its great RULER, he alike rebels
Who ferioufnefs, and pious dread repels,
    And awelefs gazes on the faded Clime,
    Dim in the gloom, and pale in the hoar rhyme,
    That o'er the bleak, and dreary Profpect fteals.
Spring claims our tender, grateful, gay delight;
    Winter our fympathy, and facred fear;
    And fure the Hearts that pay not Pity's rite
O'er wide Calamity,—that carelefs hear
    Creation's wail,—neglect, amid her blight,
    The folemn leffon of the RUIN'D YEAR.

F I N I S.